the WEIGHT of WATer

A Carnegie Medal finalist

★ "This is a wrenching but hopeful story of displacement, loneliness, and survival. . . . Crossan's verse packs a punch as she examines the power that difference—but also determination—can wield." —*Publishers Weekly*, starred review

"Graceful, effortless verse. . . . A sweet, well-paced tale [with] a silver lining." —*SLJ*

"Poignant, powerful, just perfect." —Cathy Cassidy, author of *Gingersnaps*

"Image-rich free verse that packs an emotional punch. . . . Memorable." —*Kirkus Reviews*

"A powerful coming-of-age novel about family and discovering how to be true to yourself that is well worth reading." —*Booklist*

BOOKS BY SARAH CROSSAN

The Weight of Water
Apple and Rain
Moonrise

With Brian Conaghan
We Come Apart

the WEIGHT of WATER

SARAH CROSSAN

BLOOMSBURY

NEW YORK LONDON OXFORD NEW DELHI SYDNEY

BLOOMSBURY YA
Bloomsbury Publishing Inc., part of Bloomsbury Publishing Plc
1385 Broadway, New York, NY 10018

BLOOMSBURY and the Diana logo are trademarks of Bloomsbury Publishing Plc

First published in Great Britain in January 2012 by Bloomsbury Publishing Plc
Published in the United States of America in July 2013 by Bloomsbury Children's Books
Paperback edition published in May 2018 by Bloomsbury YA

Bloomsbury books may be purchased for business or promotional use. For information on bulk
purchases please contact Macmillan Corporate and Premium Sales Department at
specialmarkets@macmillan.com

ISBN 978-1-68119-954-2 (paperback)

The Library of Congress has cataloged the hardcover edition as follows:
Crossan, Sarah.
The weight of water / by Sarah Crossan. — 1st U.S. ed.
p.   cm.
Originally published: London : Bloomsbury, 2012.
ISBN 978-1-59990-967-7 (hardcover) • ISBN 978-1-61963-047-5 (e-book)
1. Immigrants—England—Coventry—Juvenile fiction. 2. Mothers and daughters—
Juvenile fiction. 3. Swimming—Juvenile fiction. 4. Alienation (Social psychology)—
Juvenile fiction. 5. Novels in verse. 6. Coventry (England)—Ethnic relations—Juvenile
fiction. [1. Novels in verse. 2. Immigrants—England—Fiction. 3. Mothers and daughters—
Fiction. 4. Swimming—Fiction. 5. Race relations—Fiction. 6. Coventry (England)—Fiction.
7. England—Fiction.] I. Title.
PZ7.5.C76Wei 2013   [Fic]—dc23   2012038645

Typeset by Hewer Text UK Ltd., Edinburgh
Printed and bound in the U.S.A. by Sheridan, Chelsea, Michigan
4 6 8 10 9 7 5

To find out more about our authors and books visit www.bloomsbury.com
and sign up for our newsletters.

For Mum and Dad

the
WEIGHT of
WATER

PART I

Leaving Gdańsk Główny

The wheels on the suitcase break
Before we've even left Gdańsk Główny.

Mama knocks them on some steps and
      Bang, crack, rattle—
             No more use.
                There are
                    plastic bits
      Everywhere.

It's hard for Mama carrying a suitcase
And a bulging laundry bag.

It's hard for Mama
With everyone watching.

She's shy about the laundry bag,
An old nylon one
Borrowed from Babcia.

Tata took all the good luggage
When he left us,
When he walked out
On Mama and me.

"There are clean clothes in it,"
      Mama reminds me,

Like this were something
To be proud of.

And she won't let me carry a thing
        Except
                my own
                        small bag.

"You guard our passports, Kasienka.
        Good girl, Kasienka.
        And the money.
        We'll need those pounds.
Mind the money and the passports.
        Good girl, Kasienka."

Mama prattles as I scuttle along
        behind her
Dodging business suits and
        backpacks.

There is no one to recognize Mama
In the crowded station.

But all the same, she is shy
About that laundry bag.

"Now keep close, Kasienka.
        Keep close,"

Mama mutters as we leave Gdańsk Główny
And step aboard a bus for the airport

While I cling to the belt of her coat,
Too old for holding hands,
Even if she had one free.

Stansted

We weren't on a ship.
Immigrants don't arrive on
Overcrowded boats anymore,
Swarming wet docks like rats.
It isn't 1920, and it isn't Ellis Island—
Nothing as romantic as a view of
Lady Liberty
To welcome us.

We flew into Stansted.
    Not quite London
    But near enough.

At immigration we line up
Nervously and practice English in our heads:
    Yes-thank-you-officer.
I know I am not at home
When talking makes my tummy turn
And I rehearse what I say
Like lines from a play
Before opening my mouth.

At the baggage claim
The laundry bag
Coasts around the carousel
And people look.

Someone points,
So Mama says, "Leave it, Kasienka.
There's nothing in that bag but long
underwear.
We won't need them here.
We'll need galoshes."

Mama is right:
The air in England is swampy,
The sky a gray blanket.
And rain threatens
To drench us.

Dwellings

Mama rented a room
        In Coventry.

This is where we'll live
Until we find Tata:
One room on the fourth floor
Of a crumbling building
That reminds me of history class,
Reminds me of black-and-white photographs
Of bombed-
        out
            villages.

There is a white kitchen in the room,
                    In the corner,
And one big bed,
Lumpy in the middle
Like a cold pierogi
For Mama and me to share.
"It's just one room," I say,
When what I mean is,
        We can't live here.
"It's called a *studio*,"
        Mama tells me,
As though a word
Can change the truth.

Mama stands by the dirty window
With her back to me
Looking out at the droning traffic,
The Coventry Ring Road.

Then she marches to the kitchen and
Plugs in the small electric kettle.
She boils the water
Twice,
And makes two mugs of tea.
One for her,
            One for me.
"Like home," she says,
Sipping the tea,
Staring into its blackness.

Mama found the perfect home for
A cast-off laundry bag.
Yes.
But not a home for us.

First Day

Mrs. Warren asks, "Do you speak English, dear?"
Crouching down,
        Resting her hands on her knees
As though summoning a spaniel.

Her voice is loud
And clear,
Her tongue pink
        and rolling.

I nod and Mrs. Warren smiles,
Then sighs,
Relieved.

"So what's your name, dear?" Mrs. Warren asks,
And I'm glad, because I was afraid she had mistaken
Me for someone called Dear,
And that I would have to
Respond to that name
Forever.

"My name is Kasienka," I say,
    embarrassed to use my
    crooked English.

Mrs. Warren stands up straight
    and stretches her back.

She sighs,
    Again,
And ridges appear on her brow.
She looks at Mama,
        then back at me.

"Well . . . Cassie, welcome!"

I want to point out her mistake,
Give her a chance to say my
Name properly.

But Mama touches my shoulder.
        A clear caution.
"We'll start you in sixth grade
And see how that goes."

Sixth Grade

I am twelve.
Almost thirteen.
I have budding breasts and
Monthly bleeds,
But I am in a class with
Eleven-year-olds.

Mama isn't troubled.
Until I learn to read
Austen in the original
I should stay with the
Younger ones, she says.

But Mama is wrong.
Some of them have never even heard of Austen.

I understand numbers
Better than anyone in sixth grade.
The planets too.

In lessons I have to
Hide my face
With a book
So teachers
Don't see my tonsils
When I yawn.

I don't read well
In English.
That is all I can't do.

So they put me in with eleven-year-olds.

The Bell

There is a bell,
A pealing chime to signal
When everyone moves.
We are ruled by its shrillness.
Like sleepwalkers we stand
When it clangs
And return to silence
At its command.
Teachers try to lead the processions:
"*I* will decide when the lesson ends," they insist.
But they cannot compete
With The Bell.

What I Try Not to Hear

Polish words bounce about the classroom
And it should feel good to hear them but
I try not to listen;
Two boys in my class are saying things a girl
Should not hear
If she is any kind of
Lady.

They laugh, loudly, because the teacher
Is right there listening,
Not understanding,
Thinking they are being
Good
When really they are being
Horrible,
When really they are talking about
Her chest.

Konrad winks and wields his tongue
As though he would like to lick me.

But he is only eleven; he is doing his best
To shock,
And I know that if I flirted with him
Even a little,
He would probably be
Terrified.

Pale

The brown children
Play with the white children.
The black children
Play with the brown children.
They charge at one another
Hands up, like antlers,
Hitting and howling.

I'm not welcome to play.
The reason: I'm too white.

No one likes too-white,
Eastern white,
Polish-winter white,
Vampire-fright white.

Brown is okay—usually.
But white is too bad.

At lunchtime
I hide
        In the corner
        Of the yard
By a drinking fountain
Hoping only to be

Left alone.

It's the best to hope for
Among all the raised antlers.

Mute

Mama took a job
In a hospital.

Until we find Tata
We will be poor.
We will need the money.

Mama's job is to clean and carry.
She doesn't have to speak to
Anyone.

Mama's long vowels scare
The older patients.
They'd prefer to hear
A familiar, imperial voice
Than know a Pole is
Bringing them breakfast.

On her first day
A woman with crust on her face
Asks Mama where she's from,
And when Mama tells her,
The crusty creature snarls and says,
"I'd like someone English,"
Politely adding, "*Please.*"

Mama doesn't have to speak to
Anyone,
Usually.

In fact, they would rather she didn't.

She just has to clean and carry.

"Please."

Search Engine

Mama goes to the library
To check the Internet.

She thinks
Google might know where
Tata is.

But it doesn't.

When she types in Tata's name,
Google spits back
Thousands of hopeless links.

Poor Mama is too tired to cook
When she returns from her
Trip to the library,
So I make dinner:
Oatmeal with raisins and honey.

We eat in stodgy silence,
Ignoring each other
As best we can
In the small room,
Though I don't know why.

At ten o'clock
Mama lets me have the bed

To myself,
Then trickles in
An hour later.
Her feet are cold,
And she is shivering.

Mama sniffs.
"Are you sick, Mama?"

She doesn't speak.
She pretends to be asleep.

But as a car trundles by outside,
I make out, in the gloom,
The flash of a tear
On the side of Mama's face.
And though I want to console her,
I can't think how,
Without making her mad.

Noise

There are nasty people in our building.
Mama tells me not to talk to
      Anyone,
Or look at
      Anyone,
Especially when she's at work.

If they stop me on the stairs,
Or try to get into the room,
I'm to pretend I don't speak English
"Because there are nasty people here."

They are not English people.
English people do not live in this building—
It could not be home for them
Because they wouldn't fit here,
In a place infested with aliens.

Sometimes we hear children squalling
And small dogs barking,
Then yelping and whining
Long into the night.
A man shouts:
      MUTT. MUTT.

And I wonder if he is shouting
At a dog or a child.

One night a barbarian knocks
When Mama is singing.
> Her eyes are shut
> And she jumps
> When the pounding fist
> Thunders against the door.

"No noises!" he shouts.
"Against rules here!"

Mama storms to the door,
Opens it, brandishing her sheet music—
The Barber of Seville—
To prove her singing
Isn't noise.
"Against house rules!"
The man shouts again,
> His face a knot.

Mama gasps,
Presses a hand to her heart
And bangs the door
> > > Shut.

She isn't afraid of him,
> As I am;
> She's shaken
> By his ignorance.
"No noises," she repeats quietly.

As Mama starts to put away
The sheet music
I say,
        "No, Mama, sing quietly.
        For me."

And I sit up on the kitchen counter
To hear her soaring Rosina,
And remember Mama as she was,
Poised and powerful,
Lungs that could cut glass.
Before Tata left.
Before Coventry.

We hear nasty people every night
Cursing Christ and
        All the saints in heaven.
Mama blesses herself,
Showers the room in holy water
And insists I say my prayers,

Which I do,
Hiding underneath the feather duvet
Hoping God will hear me
Here
In Coventry.

Before England

Mama pitched a coffee cup
      At the wall.
Tata shouted:
"Are you crazy?
Are you? Crazy!"

Babcia picked up the pieces
As usual,
And mopped up the coffee.

Mama stamped her way
To the pantry to
      Knead dough.

Tata turned up the television.

I had two parents then,
But I couldn't be in two places,
So I sat with Babcia,
Away from them both.

Mama showed me the note from Tata
The day he disappeared.

Ola, I have gone to England

Is all he wrote.

I got no note.

And no mention in the one to Mama.

Mama cried for two whole years.
And Babcia held her all this time.
I didn't cry, even though Tata forgot me,
Even though I had a right to cry.

Babcia said, "He didn't leave *you*, Kasienka."
Which was a lie.

Because he didn't take me with him.

She just meant, *Behave yourself—*
I'm dealing with your mother.

Then a check came from Tata,
In an envelope
With a clear postmark.
And Mama knew what to do.

Now we share a damp bed
In a strange place.

Mama is still crying.
But Babcia isn't here to hold her.
And my arms are too short for the job.

Rain

It rains relentlessly.

> Rain
> Rain
> Rain.
> > All.
> > Day.
> > Long.

It is in my knuckles and my knees—
The damp.

And I've no galoshes
Or rain boots to wear.
So I wear my snow boots to school
To keep my feet dry.

The other children stare.

But I don't care.
> At least my feet are dry.

Mama says, "Don't worry, Kasienka,
They have summers here too."

But I don't know
About that.

Swimming

Mama pays,
Reluctantly:
Presses two coins into my palm
As though she's passing me a secret.

Tata taught me to swim.
Taught me to be strong.
It was no good grumbling
Or wrinkling my nose
Or crying—like a girl—
Tata didn't care about that.

"Kick your legs
From the hip,
Not the feet.
Now climb toward me
With your arms."

After swimming, Tata
Bought me ice cream:
Blueberry in a cup,
"For my Olympian."

I never want to
Paddle and play in the pool.
I'm here to work hard.
Do laps.

Up and
       Down,
              Up and
                     Down,
The power of my own body
Fluent, fluid,
Propelling me forward
Like a stone from
A slingshot.

A boy from my school is here.
A boy from eighth grade,
I think.

He is perched on the edge of the diving board
Watching me.
Up and
       Down,
              Up and
                     Down.
And when I am below him
At the deep end,
He gets up, raises his arms,
And like a hunting hawk
Plunges into the water
Effortlessly.

Surfacing, he bobs about
Gazing again.

So I swim fast,
To outswim his stare
And make Tata proud,
Even though there'll be no
Blueberry ice cream
Today.

I don't know the diving boy,
The gawking hawk boy.
But he is in eighth grade.

And he is older than me.

Disco

A poster in the classroom
Announces a dance.
A disco.
For sixth grade.

Everyone's excited.
And *everyone's* going.
Everyone but me.

For three reasons:
I'm twelve.
Almost thirteen.
Not eleven.

Deceiver

In the City Arcade
There is a shop where
Each item is one pound.

They sell everything
In that shop
For one pound.
Just one pound.

There are bags of chocolate for one pound.
And orange Halloween decorations.
They sell fairy wings
And baseballs.
It's astounding:
Everything one pound!

Mama picks up a box,
Turns it over in her hands.
It is just one pound.
But after inspection Mama
Puts it down, slowly,
And moves to the cashier
To pay for my socks and underwear.
It is a box of makeup—

Creams and powder shades:
For eyes and lips and cheeks.

In my pocket I have five bucks
Babcia gave me
Before I left.
And I want to buy Mama
The big box of makeup
She can't afford
Or pay for my own socks.

But I want the five pounds too.

I want the five pounds more.

I make a fist around the bill in my coat pocket.

"Good girl, Kasienka," Mama says.

Mama says, "Good girl, Kasienka,"
Every day.

Even when I'm not so good.

Road Atlas

Mama found a map
In a shop called
The British Heart Foundation.
She says:
    "Tata is somewhere in this city,
    And we are going to find him."
She speaks like an officer
Commanding a line of troops—
Forgetting we are only two
And presuming I wish to enlist.

She unfolds the map
Across the floor
To prepare a plan of attack,
Flattens it carefully
And says:
    "This is where we live,"
And points, with a pencil,
To an empty space.
    "How lucky we are,
    Kasienka, love.
    So close to Tata.
    He *is* here. Somewhere."

Mama looks up and I clap gently,
Fraudulently applaud her project,

While my insides tighten at one question:
What happens if we find him?

Mama waves the pencil over the map
And it flutters from the movement in the air,
As her heart must flutter
Whenever she thinks of Tata.

I wish my heart did that
       When I thought of him.

Or anyone.

But there is no space
In my belly for butterflies.

The Odyssey

Mama makes me knock and
        I inch forward
To tap lightly—
        Once.

But when Mama tuts
I knock again.
Once.
        Twice.
                Harder
                This time.

A shirtless man appears.
He shakes his head, wags a furious finger.
"No," he growls. "Whatever it is you want."

Mama prods me.
Pushes me forward—
Me and my English.

"We are looking for a man,"
Is all I can say
Because I am mesmerized by the puffy nipples.

"Do I look queer to you?
Get lost. Go on!"

He slams the door
In my face.
 Just once.
 HARD.

"What's 'queer,' Mama?" I ask.
"A type of landlord, Kasienka," Mama says,
Very sure of her English.

II

The old lady wants to help.
She looks sorry
For not knowing more,
Tells us she will ask her friends
At Tuesday bingo
If they've seen Tata.

Her head rolls to one side,
Heavy with regret,
And this makes me feel

Very small.

III

There is no answer
At the next house,
Just drawn curtains

And a closed wooden door
With the paint peeling.

IV

When it gets dark,
I want to go home.
"One more street, Kasienka,
Then home. I'll make bigos," she says.
But Mama misunderstands.
When I say home, I don't mean
The Studio.

V

She is too tired to make the bigos,
And throws together cheese sandwiches
For dinner instead.

Then she unfolds her map
And marks the streets we have searched.
"It could take us forever," I complain,
Though not too loudly,
For fear of pinching Mama's mood.
"You in a hurry to be somewhere else?"
Mama asks,
And goes back to the map,
Leaving me to my pessimism and
French homework.

Kanoro

Kanoro lives in our building.
In the next room.
He shares a bathroom with Mama and me.
But he is not a nasty person:
     He is beautiful.

He is blacker than anyone I have ever met.
     Skin like
     Wet ink.
And he scares me,
Until he smiles:
     Pink,
     All gums,
A smile that makes his eyes twinkle.

In Kenya he was a doctor.
"For children," he explains.
Again the smile,
     The gums.
     The twinkle.
In Coventry he is a janitor
At a hospital,
Like Mama.
"I like to work in hospitals," Kanoro says.

Mama laughs:
     "They think you are nothing,

These receptionist women and porter men.
But you are better than them;
You are a doctor,
And they don't know it.
Ignorant English."

Kanoro shakes his head
And like stars at dawn
The twinkle disappears.
"It is Kanoro who is ignorant,
If he thinks he is better.
There is honor in all things," he says.

Mama winces, then smiles.
And in her smile there is an
                    Inky glint.

When I Go Swimming Again

The staring boy is there,
Sitting on the tiles
With his feet in the water.
        Kicking.

I hurry to the other end of the pool,
        Head down,
        Hands hiding my chest,
        Planning to dive in,
        To save myself.

But somehow I stumble
                    And fall,
Making a mighty

            SPLASH

That attracts too much attention.

Mistaken

When Mama said,
"We're going to England,"

I didn't see myself

Alone.

I knew I'd be different,
Foreign.
I knew I wouldn't understand
Everything.

But I thought, maybe, I'd be exotic,

Like a red squirrel among the gray,

Like an English girl would be in Gdańsk.

But I am not an English girl in Gdańsk.
I'm a Pole in Coventry.

And that is not the same thing
At all.

Group Work

Five foreigners in my class
And, very strange,
Quite coincidentally,
Teachers never put us
To work in the same groups.

Each group must be given
Its fair share of duds.
No need to overburden
One particular person.

This isn't prejudice:
None of the smart ones
Ever end up together,
None of the dumb kids either,
Or the noisy, naughty ones.

Teachers aren't stupid.
But maybe they think we are,
When they pretend to make
Random selections.

The teachers who *do* let us choose
Make the mistake of thinking
Everyone will find a place.

But there are always

One or two of us,
Left sitting,
        Desperately scanning,
Hoping to be considered
By a group of unpopulars
With too few people
Before the teacher turns,
Detects the exclusion,
And with a wagging finger says,
        "*You!* Work with *them*."

There is eye rolling and chair scraping
As we shuffle forward,
Unwanted and misused,
Like old boots dragged
From a river.

William

The boy from the swimming pool,
The boy from eighth grade,
    The watcher,
Is called William.

He tells me I'm a mean swimmer
And should be on the school team.

I didn't know there was a team,
But I should be on it,
    William says.
I'm mean,
    William says,

Pushing his hair
    Out of his eyes
    And hitching up his jeans
Which are slipping around his hips.

He doesn't say much more—
    He just stares,
And this staring brings my dinner
Back into my throat:
Green beans and bacon.

I swallow it quickly.
And with twisted tongue tell him

I'm twelve,
Almost thirteen,
In case he thinks otherwise.

When I talk he looks at me
Like I am amazing,
And then he says,
"*Why* are you in sixth grade?"
And I don't want him to think
I'm stupid, so I have to say,
"It's because I'm Polish.
I'm in sixth grade because
I'm Polish."

This is the truth
And yet, it is only
A small piece
Of it.

Small Secrets

I tell Mama about the swim team
But not about William.

"No time for this, Kasienka,"
Mama says. "We have to find Tata."
She points to the map
Pinned to the wall like ugly art.

I nod, *yes*, though I do not want to look for Tata—
Tata does not want to be found;
He is in hiding—he is hiding from us both,
A truth that makes me grind my teeth sometimes.
But I don't tell Mama this,
Even when we're searching.
Night after night,
      Street after street,
            One door at a time,
                  And it's raining,
                        And I'm hungry,
                            And teary,
                            And tired.
Because hope is all Mama has.
And I cannot take it from her.

Drip Tap

There is a leaky tap in the kitchen,
    in our room, where we sleep.

All night it plays a rapping rhythm
    against the metal sink,
And Mama, next to me,
    murmurs along to its beat.

I want to get out of bed to tighten the tap,
    stop the dripping—the rapping-tapping.
It's times like these Tata would be useful.
    He'd have a box of tools
And no fear about waking Mama
    to get the tap fixed,
      though she might grumble.

Meal Times

He uses sharp spices
Which we taste in our dinner
        Through the walls.

Mama invites Kanoro
To eat with us,
To share our evenings.
Sometimes he brings his bright rice with him.
And he always brings his smile and

        Twinkling eyes.

Wanted

Mama is wasting money
We don't have.
She prints posters
With Tata's picture on them
And the word *MISSING.*

She makes one hundred copies
On purple paper,
So people will notice them
Stapled to the trees
Around Coventry.

They are like wanted posters,
But Tata is not a criminal.
They are like posters people
Put up when they've lost a cat,
But Tata is not an animal.

I'm embarrassed for him
In case he *is* living in Coventry
And doesn't want to be found—
Like some criminal or animal.

When we've put up
      half the posters
I tell Mama
          it's enough.

Her mouth becomes a hard line.
She snatches the pile of papers from me.

"Kasienka, do you know
That you are useless?" she snaps.

The answer to this question is
        YES:
I know.
I am useless.

Examinations

They have come up with a
Civil way for saying we are slow,
But it all means the same thing:

I get extra time because
I have *special needs*.

No one wants to be special at school.
I simply want to be the same as everyone else.
No one wants to have special needs.

In the math exam I don't need the extra time—
Finishing the paper is as easy as
Finishing a plateful of raspberries.
I have an hour left over,
Which annoys the monitor
Marking his own exams.
"Read over your workings," he grumps.
But I don't.

I don't need to read over
                              Anything.

Because I don't have special needs.

And I'm not eleven.

Novice

I teach Kanoro chess.
He doesn't even know
Where the pieces sit.

So we take our time
Setting up the board,
Making our moves,
Watching for mistakes
And ignoring the clock.

We are competitive,
And we are generous.

Kanoro wins game three—
       Checkmate.
He laughs, his mouth a wide
Sunlit cavern.

And Mama laughs too,
Lips barely parted,
Her nostrils giving it away,
And her eyes, which,
For a moment,
Lower their longing,
And seem to see
Me clearly.

Mama offers to restore
The family pride—
Takes my seat
And lines up her troops.

"I'm a lucky man," Kanoro says,
Looking closely at the squares
On the chessboard.

And I don't know if he's
Talking about his win

Or something else entirely.

Christmas

Babcia arrives carrying two heavy suitcases,
Though she's only staying one week.

She doesn't like Coventry
                         At all:
It's too warm to be winter and
No one speaks Polish.
"Why don't they try?" Babcia bleats.

Mama points a finger at Babcia—
"You don't speak English, Mama.
Only a little Russian.
Why don't *you* try?"

Babcia sniffs—
        "I'm an old woman," she says,
        and Mama smiles.

Babcia tells Mama to come home.
"For the New Year concerts.
For the skiing."
Mama turns her back on Babcia
And continues with the cooking.
Babcia sings as she sews,
Old parsnip fingers guiding the thread.

She quilts patchwork bedcovers
From old shirts and skirts—
Clothes no one wants
Babcia turns into magic.

Kanoro comes to dinner
On Christmas Eve
And Babcia shrieks—
"So, so black!"
                    In Polish of course.
Mama frowns and we sit to eat.

We sing carols,
Eat boiled ham,
Open small boxes
Wrapped with bows,

And it is good enough.

Mama's Mama

In Poland, Mama and Babcia
Didn't argue. They were on the
Same side.

                      The opposite side
                      To Tata.

In England, Mama gets prickly
Whenever Babcia
Mentions Tata
Or complains about him.
Mama gets prickly about
A lot of things.

                      She won't let Babcia
                      Help in the kitchen
                      With the cooking,
                      Won't let her mend the curtains
                      Which are ripped and frayed,
                      Or take me shopping
                      For new swim goggles.
"She's *my* daughter.
I can buy her what she needs,"
Mama says, though this is a lie.
Mama is always annoyed with Babcia,
But Babcia hasn't done anything wrong
                      That I can see.

The night before Babcia leaves

I am in Kanoro's room
Watching television
When the squabbling seeps through the wall.

> *"You must think of the child, Ola.*
> *You come back to Poland*
> *When you find him.*
> *It isn't fair on the child.*
> *Let me take her home."*

"Her home is with me, Mama.
I can take care of her. Don't
You see how happy she is?"

> *"Are you blind, you mule?*
> *You live in a dump.*
> *Her only friend is that black man."*

"He is a good man."

> *"You don't know him."*

"He is a doctor."

> *"You are pigheaded."*

"Pigheaded, Mama,
Is better than old
And ignorant."

"Lord have Mercy!"

I shoot Kanoro a look,
Embarrassed,
Wishing he hadn't heard,
Wishing the walls were stronger,
When I remember he can't
Understand the Polish they are using.
And I am grateful.

        I do not want to go back to the
           room.
        I do not want to choose
Between Mama
        And Babcia.

But when dinner is ready
Mama knocks on the wall, as usual,
And there is no more
Quarreling in the room.

        They make an excellent effort
        To pretend everything is well.

Snow Meal

When they say it might snow
I sit by the window,
My fingertips pressed against glass,
Waiting.

I know it's childish,
But I want to
Build a tubby snowman,
  A man with button eyes
And a long carrot nose.

Kanoro watches with me;
He's never seen snow
And never built a snowman,
So we'll make it
  Together—
And it will remind me of home
For the few hours it lives.

When they say it might snow
We sit by the window,
Our fingertips pressed against glass,
Waiting.

Suddenly a scattering
Of children emerges
And dance to silent music
Together in the street.

A few flakes are falling.
They melt into the ground
Like stones thrown into a lake.

Kanoro pulls on my elbow.
"Let's go. It's snow!" he says.

There isn't enough settling to
Make a snowman's big toe,
Even if we collected all the snow
In the street.

Kanoro rushes to his room
And returns wearing
A thick woolen coat,
Though there's no need for it;
No chance of real snow landing.

Outside Kanoro opens his mouth
To taste the snowflakes.
And I do the same.

A cool dusting fills
My mouth with memories
Of winter.

We look up at the night sky
And eat our snow meal.

Change

The exams have been marked
After the break
And Mrs. Warren admits her mistake:
So I start seventh grade
Where I should have been
All along.

Again,
No one talks to me
    At all.

So I sit
    On my own
At the front of the classroom
Furiously trying to keep up
With the bored teachers
Who don't seem
To notice I'm new.

In assembly I spot William.
He nods, a secret salute,
Then sits on the opposite side of the hall
Next to a boy with big teeth
And a thin mustache.

And I spend assembly
Pretending not to look at him.

Happy Slapping

In science, Clair shows me
Her mobile phone and on it
A video
     Of an attack
     On a boy
     At a bus stop.

Not for money.
Not for revenge.
Not really for fame either—
It's just for fun:
To see someone
Suffer.
     Slapped.

I look up and laugh
Sheepishly,
And Clair approves—
"I'll send it to you,"
She promises,
Then shepherds the phone to
The row behind
     So they too can
Feast on
The fun.

I do not mention
I have no phone.

Games

They pick teams and I am not last
To be picked because Clair chooses me.

Clair chooses me third out of six girls
And I am on her team for softball.

I can catch, and I can hit, and I can run
And when I do she squeals, "Go, Cassie! Go!"

And afterward, when we are getting changed
She says, "The other team was crap!"

And I wasn't on the other team.

Radio News Flash

A Croatian builder was attacked
last night in Birmingham
on his way home from work
with his own hammer . . .

Three fourteen-year-old youths
are now in custody awaiting bail . . .

Witnesses say the attackers shouted
"Give us back our jobs, Polack!"
before bludgeoning his skull
with the forged-steel head . . .

The thirty-year-old father from Moseley,
now in the Birmingham Specialist Unit,
is said to be in critical but stable condition . . .

Mama puts a piece of
Potato into her mouth
But doesn't chew.
Kanoro looks at her
Meaningfully.
What do meaningful looks mean anyway?

Prize Night Envy

It takes two hours to honor those smarter than us
And watch them parade across the polished stage
To receive award
                    after award.

Mama sits with the other parents.
She looks puzzled because I'm not called
Forward for a medal or a trophy.
I don't even get a certificate she can
Stick to the fridge.

Clair is sitting next to me
Defacing the program.
She sneers when other people win
And groans instead of clapping.

There are sports awards.
William wins a swimming medal—gold—
        And when he sits
Back down he passes the medal
Along our row so I can touch it.

Stabbing jealousy makes my head spin,
And then there's guilt in my gut
Because William looks so proud,
And he has been so nice;
He deserves this medal.

I pass it back along the row
And Clair turns to me and asks,
"You're friends with Will?"
And I shrug;
        I don't think we are friends,
        Exactly.

For the finale we stand in our rows
Like disheveled soldiers
And sing "God Save the Queen."

I don't know the words.
I just open and close my
Mouth and look straight ahead
Hoping no one will notice
The treason.

Anyone Else

I am the best runner in the class.
It's not arrogance, it's a fact:
When I'm on a team
                    We win.

But Clair doesn't pick me anymore.
She looks past me,
                    Through me
To anyone else.

Instead of me
She chooses Bella
       who won't bat because she has her period,
And Rachel
       who can't run because she forgot her sneakers.

She chooses girls who won't catch
               or race
               or jump
Because they just
Can't be bothered.

Then I am the last one standing
So Clair has no choice;
She has to take me.

And I am on her team,

But I know this makes her
                            Mad
Because she rolls her eyes
And whispers something
To Marie that I can't hear.

But she wants me to see her whispering,
        Of course.

When we play I am told
To field,
                            Way back
                            By the bushes
Where the ball
Never falls.
And when I bat
No one cheers anymore.
No one cares that I get a home run.
Only when I'm tagged
                            OUT
Are they satisfied.

In the Dark

The worst thing:
I don't even know
What I did wrong.

Another thing:
I'm meant to know
What I did wrong
And fix it.

Clair says, "Don't worry about it,"
But I do.
How can I forget it
When she won't let me?

Time to Grow

Girls in England
Have long hair.
Hair that's flat
And sits neatly
On their shoulders.

My hair is short
And black,
And sticks up in
The morning
Like moody fur.

The girls in my class
Speak to me, finally.
And Clair asks about my hair—
Why it's short.

"Is it because you're really a boy?"
She wants to know.

It's true that
Some boys have
Longer hair than me.

So, I decide to grow it.
And wear a flower in it,

So I won't look
Like a Polish boy
Anymore.

All Wrong

Today I was told
I have the wrong bag.
Today I was told that
My bag is *ridiculous.*

I have looked carefully
At the offending bag.

It's an ordinary backpack
For school books,
With sections
For smaller items.

Today I was told
It is *all wrong.*

I'm looking at the bag.
I'm desperate to know
What doesn't work.
But I just can't figure it out.

Karma

If I were back in Gdańsk, I wouldn't be friends
With a new girl either.
If I still had Magdalena
To copy homework from
And sit with at lunch,
I'd ignore a new girl too,
Like we snubbed Alexsandra who stood
Far enough away
To be discreet.
Close enough to be invited.

We just ignored her.

We played tennis, pretended not to notice
She was holding a racket and
Wearing shorts with pockets.
Why did we do that?

But we weren't mean to her.
We didn't whisper and laugh,
Avoid touching her in case we caught something.

We simply ignored her.

If I Were on the Swim Team They Might See Me

Sometimes I want to tear off my clothes
And show them I'm the same
           Underneath—
           Maybe better.

It doesn't matter what I wear.
I always look different:
My clothes are too heavy—
That much I can tell.
And I have no real vision,
I just don't see what's wrong.

If I were on the swim team
I'd wear a swimsuit
Like everyone else,
There'd be more skin than fabric.

If I were on the swim team,
They might see me.

Name Day

As I rub away cold sleep,
Mama pulls out a box
Wrapped in starry blue paper,
    A card taped to the top—
Kasienka on it
In neat script.

I sit up in the bed
And rip open the paper.

Mama cheers: "Your own iron!"

I want to stop unwrapping.
I want to cry.

What do I need an iron for?
    We already have one, which leaks,
    like the tap
    in the kitchen.

When I take the box out of its wrapping
I see Mama's mistake—or mine—
It's a hair iron,
"A straightener," I say,
Genuinely joyful,
And read the box aloud:
        Ceramic plates.

Mama shrugs. I shrug.
We don't know if *ceramic plates* is good—
    It sounds good,
      Printed in bold, square letters.

Later on, after we've lunched on fresh golabki,
And I've straightened my hair,
Mama, Kanoro, and I march to the cinema.
We gorge on sweet buttered popcorn and
      Orange sodas.

We sit in the front row, me in the middle,
Smiling all the way
Through a sad film.

The Hunt

They don't have to say
         a thing.
They just have to stare
At my hair,
For me to know
It isn't enough
To impress them,
Though it's so straight now
You could paint with it.

Clair confirms that
It is still too short,
I still look like a boy—

"Are you a boy?"

A paper appears in my locker.

FYI: *You smell like old meat.*

I hurry to the toilets to sniff myself,
And when I'm there,
Clair and Marie arrive
With a gaggle of girls.

"Can you smell something?"
Clair wonders,

And Marie holds her nose,
And then the other girls do too.

They are hunting,
Circling me to prevent my escape.
They yap and snuffle,
Jostle to be close to Clair,
Covering their mouths
To stifle laughter.

I am a fox surrounded by beagles.
They will eat me alive and spit out the fat.

I am their prey and there is nothing
I can do to stop them pouncing.

Maybe

Leaning on the lockers,
Chewing on a straw,
Clair pretends she can't
See me because she's
     Alone—
Without the pack.

I close my locker loudly,
With a
     BANG
And for a second she shudders
Then turns
And shows off her braces.

"Hi, Cassie!" she says,
Blinking.

That's all.
And I wonder if
This means
We're friends.

Art Class

A shadow frowns over my craft paper,
And then a warm voice: "That's good, Cassie."
Arlene puts her picture down next to mine.
She's slight, with round glasses that hide
                              half her face.

We sit together using our thumbs
To blend chalk dust into
Fat green cucumbers,
And I think, maybe she's the one,
Maybe she's the friend
I've been waiting to find.

But Clair tracks me down at the sink
Where we go to wash the colors from
Our hands.

"Is it true what you said about Arlene?"

I gaze at Clair,
Too amazed to protest.
Arlene looks sideways at me.
She wipes her hands on her trousers

And backs away from the
Danger of friendship.

"Arlene's a bit sensitive,"
Clair hisses and slinks away too.

Nothing more.

In the sink the colors have washed away,
And the water runs clear.

Not Alone

William finds me in the cafeteria.
He moves to my table, drops his tray,
And sits.

He slurps and burps,
Wipes his mouth on his sleeve
And stares.

Eighth-grade boys watch us
From across the hall.
They are gesturing,
                    Guffawing.
"My friends," William says,
"Are idiots."

And then, "You haven't been to practice."
I shake my head and sip my Coke.
I know it's better when I don't talk.
"So maybe I'll see you at the pool this week.
Maybe you'll be there on Thursday," he says.

He waits for me to speak.
I nod and
Dip my fries
In ketchup.

"So you'll be there on Thursday,"
He says.

Walking to science he takes my hand
    And squeezes it
As though testing a piece of fruit in a market
    Before buying.

Then he puts his hands into his trouser pockets
And says, "I'll see you at the pool then.
Thursday."

Thursday

In the changing room
I check myself in the mirror.
I want to be sure
I look normal.

I do not:
I am sharp cornered,
Like a piece of Swedish
                    Self-assembly furniture
                        Gone wrong.
I am all lines,
No curves.

My fingers and toes are too long.
My nose is pointy, my bottom flat.

When did this happen?

I tiptoe to the pool,
My towel hiding my shape.

Apart from a lone lifeguard
Sitting in what looks like
A baby's high chair
The place is deserted.

I cannot see William anywhere.

I drop the towel and let the water
      Take me.

And I do laps:
Up and
      Down,
            Up and
                  Down,
Waiting for William
Who never shows up and
Trying not to think about

Rejection.

Grating

I am hairy.

I have thick
    black
    shoots
Under my arms
And on my legs
And between them too.

I am hairy.

I did not know this until
I noticed the women
In the pool
With their velvety skin.

I am hairy.

So when I get home
I swipe Mama's razor,
Sneak down to the bathroom,
And work on the problem.

I rest one hairy leg on the toilet seat
And drag the blade up it.

I scream. Loudly,

Like someone is trying to murder me
And Mama runs up the hall
And knocks on the door:
"What is happening, Kasienka?"
She wants to know.
She wants to know
I'm not being murdered.

Little red rivers
Run down to my ankles
And pool on the toilet seat.

"I'm okay, Mama," I say.

I have not shaved the hair
But grated the skin.

There is pink flesh
In the blade,
No hair at all.

When I emerge from the bathroom
I am still hairy.
And covered in cuts.

What William Says

I wanted to call you
But I didn't have your number.
If I had your number
I would have called
For sure
You know.

I was really sick.
I was so queasy
I couldn't eat.
I couldn't get out of bed.
I had a stomach bug, the doctor said.

Anyway,
If I'd had your number
I would have called
For sure
You know.

Sorry I didn't show up
At the pool.
Man, I was so sick.
But I couldn't get in touch with you.

Let's do it another time.
I won't be sick.

I'm done with sick.
You know.

For sure.

Back in Gdańsk

I dream about Tata.

We are in a train station.
Maybe we are in
        Gdańsk Główny.

People are
        Milling yet purposeful,
Like ants
        Around a sugar bowl.

Mama and I are trailing
                                Tata
Through the crowd.

He glances back,
Encouraging us.
Then disappears
                        Suddenly.

And I wake up
Soundlessly sobbing.

Finding Tata

Mama will not give up.

It is cold and drizzles most nights,
So Mama buys a scarf and umbrella,
But she will not give up.
Even as a door closes
She looks to the next one,
Each time with a sleepier smile,
But she will not give up.
Her boots need to be reheeled.
They are worn out, as I am,
From the hard pavements.
So Mama borrows my boots
Though they're a little tight,
But she will not give up.

I wish Mama would give up.
And stop dragging me around after her
Like a human dictionary.

I Wish Tata Were Dead

Dead fathers don't deliberately leave home.
They can be sainted.
We can hold candles to their memories
And keep their headstones clean.

You can't do this with a missing father.

Questions

Kanoro is in our room
Holding hands with Mama.
They look like they are praying.

Kanoro's face is moist
And his eyes are cloudy,
The stars bitten out.

Later I want to know the story,
The reason for the quiet closeness.

"Did he explain the scar on his cheek?"
Mama won't tell.
Mama says, "Always too many questions
With you."

So I decide, right then,
Never to ask her anything else ever again.

And to tell her even less.

Daredevil

Marie Mullen is the messenger:
    If I agree to do
    Three dares
    In three days,
Dares Clair will devise,
I'll be allowed to sit with
Everyone
    During lunch
        For a week
            As a trial.

I think it's a joke so I laugh.
Marie Mullen glances about—
She thinks I've seen something
Funny.

"What kinds of things?" I ask.

Marie Mullen says: "I don't know.
Take a piss on the tennis courts.
Ask a senior on a date.
Drink a quart of olive oil."

"Did you do all that?" I ask.
Marie Mullen looks away.

I'm sorry for her,
But my answer is no—

I'd rather eat alone all year
Than piss on a tennis court.
I'd rather eat alone forever
Than jump at Clair's bidding.

This is what I tell myself.

I Try to Tell Mama

And all she says is,
"Girls are like this."

As though I'm like
This too.

The Pity Club

Not all girls are savage.
Some stand away
When Clair starts.
Some turn their backs.
They won't take part.

They are The Pity Club—
The girls who look at me
With sorry eyes when
I'm the only person
Without a partner in PE.

But they have their own group,
And it's established.
      And exclusive.
      And a newbie would
      Mess it all up.

So—
      They aren't cruel.
They are The Pity Club,
And I don't know what's worse:
Pity or persecution.

Smokers' Corner

William leads me to a corner of the playground.
I pat down my hair and flatten out my skirt
Expecting to be kissed.

But when we get there it's crowded
And smoky and William doesn't kiss me.
He doesn't move any closer at all.

Marie and Clair are there.
They run their hands through their hair,
Reminding me I'm missing something.

William pulls a pack of cigarettes from
His blazer pocket and holds it out to me.
I've no choice with the girls gazing and grinning.

When I inhale it's like breathing in dirt,
The kind Mama shakes out of the rug.

William smiles, takes the cigarette from me,
Inhales, swallows, licks his lips.
Then he blows the smoke out through his nose
Like a shaman, and I am bewitched.

When I looked at William
I saw a swimmer.
Now I see a smoker.
        And it doesn't matter.

He talks easily to the girls
Because he is older and that
Means something.

Before we leave, Clair,
Watching me over his shoulder,
Kisses him on the side of his mouth.

I am speechless:
I am so jealous I want to hurt William.
Even though he didn't do the kissing
I want to pinch him. Or worse.
I hug myself so I will not harm him
And so I do not have to hold his hand
As we walk back
Across the playground.

Then he says, "So, are we meeting tomorrow?"
And I forgive him for the kiss.

Because even if Clair wants him,
I think
He wants
Me.

Oh, to Be Musical

I wish I knew how to play a complicated musical
Instrument,
Like a clarinet maybe,
Or a flute,
So I'd have practice using my mouth
                        And fingers,
                        And taking long breaths,
                        All at once
To create something
        Sweet.

I have never kissed a boy,
And even though
I've seen it done
Day after day
On television
And in films,
So it shouldn't be too difficult,

Because the movements are natural
                        And smooth.

I am not a naturally smooth person,
So how will I know what to do
When—
If he leans in with his head slightly tilted?

Should I tilt too?
And my mouth.
Should I open my mouth?

And my tongue.

Oh.

It is too much to think about.

It will be like playing a clarinet with no lessons;
It will take me years to learn this—
How to kiss.

Floating

William is at the swimming pool.
He is standing far away from me
In the shallow end,
Ripples sloshing his sides.

And he is watching me
As I cast aside my green towel
And pour myself into the
Safety of the water.

We swim to the middle
To meet each other,
Then lie on our backs
The water supporting our weight.

Sometimes our wrinkled toes touch
Accidentally.
Sometimes on purpose.
And for a moment I think it might be
The happiest I've ever been.

Until Clair surfaces from the deep end,
Like a serpent from a swamp,
And wipes away my smile
By smirking herself.

Rumors

Clair sent a text message to Marie,
And now Marie is
forwarding it
to everyone else in seventh grade.
Except me,
Because I don't
Have a phone.

Arlene shows me the message:
Guess what Cassie woz
doin with Will at the
swimming pool?!
She's nasty!

Now I'm scared to talk to William,
Or even look at him,
In case they think
It's true.

When I go to my locker,
All the girls from my class
Stop talking and
Stand with their
Arms folded,
Glaring.

Clair is there,

Of course.
      In the middle.
And she is simply smiling.

"Why won't you talk to me?"
William asks at lunch.
He is frowning
At the floor.
I can't answer.
I am ashamed
Of the rumors;
I want them to stop.

I want them to stop
More than I want him
To kiss me.

When Boys Fight

A drove of spectators circles them
Baying for bruises and blood
And chanting
Like soccer fans
Or soccer hooligans—
Fight. Fight. Fight.
And no one stops this easy entertainment—
They just sell more tickets.

When two boys fight they are like
Warring walruses:
>They plough into each other
>>Thumping and cracking,
>Faces tight, fists curled,
And they do not stop
Until there is a winner,
Until there is no more need to fight.

Sometimes it cannot end this way.
If a teacher shows up it ends when they are
>Forced
>>Apart
And taken, in all their bloody glory,
To the principal
Where they are spoken to
About fighting,

About using their fists
To settle squabbles.

And either way, it seems a better fix
Than whispers and giggles.

So maybe what I should do is
      Hit Clair—
      Knock her down
And we could brawl in the playground too,
With everyone watching.

Then people would know
I'd been in a battle.

Late Nights

There is a flu epidemic—
Old people are sick with feverish coughing,
So Mama works late; she helps nurses
Change beds, mop vomit,
Deliver meals around the wards.

For a few glorious days
We don't search the streets,
And I am grateful.

Mama asks Kanoro to watch me.

We sit on the floor in his room
Eating meat rolled in flat bread,
Guzzling tall glasses of cold milk.

Kanoro remembers stories
Of elephants and tribal chiefs.
They are myths and histories
Meant to entertain,
They are not his own truths,
        not for me.

Yet I tell him about William.
I tell him all about William and the
Tumblings in my tummy,

And he nods with a knowing
That makes me blush.

And then I speak about Tata,
Destroy the sugary fiction
Mama has tried to turn into truth.
I tell him,
"In Poland there is a saying:
     Running away makes you guilty.
I am afraid of what we will find,
Kanoro, if we ever find Tata."

And he says,
"I told Ola, I told your mother,
     Do not follow a person
     Who is running away,
But she will not listen.
She does not understand.
She loves your tata,
     I think."

Kanoro shakes his head
And offers me more peppery lamb
Which I take and eat,
Chewing on the gristle
And swallowing it.

Lifesaver

We are in an empty swimming pool.

The water is warm and for some reason
There is sun on my face.

I am in the deep end wearing floaties
To stop me going under.

William is there too.
But he isn't in the pool.
He's in the lifeguard's chair
Watching as I struggle to stay afloat.

Finally he jumps into the pool
Straight from the chair.

I'm kicking, sinking, but
He drags me to the side,
Up onto the pool's edge
And gives me mouth-to-mouth.

His lips and mine are wet
As they press together and
His breath fills me up.

I don't need resuscitation
But he has his hands on my chest

Between my breasts,
And he's pushing and pushing
Trying to jump-start my heart.

When I awake I am gasping.
Then I roll over and see Mama watching.
She's bleary eyed and half-asleep
But even so, I do not want to
Have dreams like this
Lying next to my mother.

Higher

We are in the park
On the swings

But I don't feel like a little kid
Because we are not swinging,
Just swaying.

William takes out his cigarettes
And offers me one.

This time I shake my head—no—
And he doesn't care.
He puts the cigarettes back into the recess
Of his blazer
And sways—
Not forward and back
But side to side
On the swing

So as he comes close
I can smell him.

I can smell his chewing gum.
Then he gets off his swing and starts to push me
So I am swinging
Higher and
        Higher.

And I am laughing because,
Actually,
I *do* feel like a little kid,
After all.

And I like it.

Dear William

I don't want you to write a poem for me
But it would be nice if you did.

And if you bought a rose for me
It would be okay too
But I don't want you to buy flowers
Necessarily.

I don't want you to carry my backpack
But if you feel like doing that
Spontaneously
I wouldn't stop you.

I wouldn't stop you being romantic
If that's what *you* wanted.

First Kiss

Oh God.
Oh God.

It is so embarrassing
When he tries to kiss me
And our faces collide like cars
In a traffic accident.

As he leans in
I open my mouth
Too
                    Wide
Like a yawn
And his pursed lips disappear into
The hollow of my mouth
So I feel like I am swallowing
Him.

He pulls away.
He looks at me like he
Is trying to figure out an algebra problem.

I am too difficult for him.
When he turns away,
Because he is embarrassed too,
I still have my mouth open

Yawn
               Wide
But now it's because I am in shock
From the accident
And I can't close it.

Assembly

Why would Clair
Steal a pair of scissors from the art room
And then,

Sitting behind me in assembly,
Listening to the principal
Make announcements,
Cut chunks from my hair?

I was trying to grow it.
I was trying to get it right.

Her stunt makes the other girls
Tee-hee-hee.

At least she got some *tee-hee*
Titters from it.

Later Clair apologizes,
Hands back my hair and,
With big eyes and a sticky pout says,
"Don't be like that, Cassie,
It was just a joke."

What kind of joke is this?
Maybe it's an English joke
I can't yet understand.

But I suspect I understand
Perfectly.

No Offense, But . . .

I shouldn't take things the wrong way
Because they are "just joking"
And they mean "no offense"
And they laugh—*ha-ha-ha*—
Because "not really"
Makes everything they do
Mean nothing
At all.

Wrath

I will find a way
To take revenge
On Clair,
For the hair—
And on her whispering friends too.

I will find a way
To watch with glee
As Clair
Feels despair
Along with her
Cheerleaders.

I can be angry.

Not always
Good Kasienka,
As Mama thinks.

Teachers

Why can't they see what's happening?
Why don't they notice the looks,
The smirks, the eye rolling?

And why don't they ask if I'm okay?

> I'll tell them I'm not.
> I'm not a liar.
> Or *nasty*.

Why do they always ask Clair
to pass out the books
And Marie to read her homework aloud?

They see what they want
Because if they didn't it would be a lot of work,
And they don't have time for this;

They have to mark, and teach, and stop the
Boys from killing one another
With their teeth and fists.
This is more important than spotting snickers.

But why can't they just ask if I'm okay?

Misread

I don't want to be secretive.

Mama and I share a bed.
Every night it's she and I together.

There are just some things
I can't say.

Mama isn't a good listener.

Sometimes, when I speak,
And think I've said something,
Mama hears something else
Completely.

And the reaction is unexpected.

Like last week—I asked for money
To buy a tube of mascara.

She raised an eyebrow
And tapped her tummy.

I didn't understand.

"Vulgar girls—always having babies—
Don't be one of those, Kasienka.
Be a good girl."

Now someone tell me—
How can mascara make me pregnant?

So when I come home with fresh-chopped hair
I don't tell her it was Clair in assembly
Sitting behind me with blunt scissors.

I tell her the teacher did it.
I tell her I got gum in it.
Because Mama won't understand—
And she will find a way to blame *me*.

The story makes Mama laugh:
"I told you that habit was disgusting.
But you never listen to Mama!"

Talking

Kanoro listens without saying,
    Just ignore it (which I can't),
    Or, *They're jealous* (which isn't true).
Instead he nods and says:
"There is no hyena without a friend."
And then: "What will you do?"

I like this question. He believes
I can do
Something.

So I tell him about my empty plan
To get revenge
On the hyena.

Kanoro looks sad and says:
"Happiness should be your revenge, Kasienka.
Happiness."

And though he is right,
It makes me feel worse
Because I do not know
How to be happy.

PART 2

Gummy Bears

When he tries to kiss me
I do not open my mouth at all
And neither does he.

We kiss,
      Dry lips on dry lips,
               And it is nice.

But it is not enough
And I feel my mouth open
      And his too.
And something that is not my mouth
      Is inside my mouth.

And it is easy:
Kissing William is like
having a gummy bear

In my mouth.
It is easy.

Kissing William
is just like sucking on a gummy bear.

Partners

William corrects my English.
Gently.
And smiles when I mispronounce things
Because he thinks the mistakes are cute.
And for the first time
Ever
I can be wrong
And it's okay.
Better than that—
It's cute.

And he thinks I'm clever too,
And asks for help with his
Simultaneous equations.
And when he gets something muddled
I smile
Because it's cute.

And so it's perfect.
We're partners.
Me on numbers.
Him on words.

Love Is a Large W

Love is watching
Love is waiting
Love is wanting
Love is worrying
Love is wishing
Love is willing

Love is whispers
Love is wet
Love is wordless

Love is Him
Love is Me
Love is We
Love is . . .
Love is . . .

Ah.

William.

Kenilworth Castle

We went on a school trip to Warwick Castle
But I couldn't believe in that place—
So symmetrical,
So perfectly preserved,
So clean
It reminded me of Disneyland—
What I imagine Disneyland would look like.

I could make no sense of its shine.

When I tell William he agrees.
We both think castles should be crumbling
After all those years,
To prove they've seen
Real history.
And history is struggle
And war,
We think.

So he takes me to Kenilworth
On the bus with him.
To see the ruins in the rain.

Elizabeth
Kept her favorite here,
In Kenilworth.

And Time stood still when she came:
The Great Clock Tower
Stopped
For her
And they feasted and frolicked,
Elizabeth and her favorite—
Right here.

And it is the most romantic place I've ever seen:
Kenilworth Castle continuing to
Crumble, as it should,
    in the rain.

Lottery

Kanoro slumps on the stone steps
Of our old building
Clasping a piece of paper
In his fist
Like it's a losing lottery ticket.

He pats the step
Inviting me to sit too.

We watch the traffic,
      The women pushing strollers and
            The gangs in hoods.
I can tell from his silence that
Kanoro holds a heavy confession.

I think he wants to reveal the terrible tale,
The one he told Mama,
The horrible one I can't know.

But it's worse than that.

It's Tata.

"Your father's address," he says,
Slipping me the paper
He's been holding.

I take it,
Afraid to look,
Though I don't know why.

"Go alone, Kasienka.
Don't take Mama Ola."

"Is Tata alive?" I ask.
Kanoro nods *and* shakes his head.
Which might mean
Tata's half-dead,
Or should be.

Ending the Odyssey

The driver won't reopen the doors
Once they're closed,
Even when a man runs
To catch up
And raps on the glass
Begging to be admitted.

The driver doesn't even look
Across at the man,
At the closed door.
He acts like he can't hear him,
But we all can.

Someone has smeared something red
Across the window of the bus.
It smells of tomato.
It may have been a
Piece of pizza.

The woman next to me
Keeps muttering to herself
And laughing.
The children at the back
Shout at a passerby,
Words in a mixing bowl.

I ring the bell,

A small red button
On the metal post,
And in my head a booming
As I signal *stop*,
And in my heart a bomb.

When the driver slows
And pulls over,
I consider sitting back down
Next to the muttering woman
And the smeared window,
And getting off at a different stop
Where there's nothing to unravel.

And no answers to fear.

The Bungalow

A woman opens the door
To the squat house.
She is wearing slippers
And a pink dressing gown
Though it is still light out.

She is distracted by a noise inside,
The sound of a small child crying.
She turns away for a moment
And then looks at me again.

I tell her my name.
And some of my story.

She ushers me in:
She wants me to meet the child
And wait for Tata.

Cold Hot Chocolate

I know the sound of Tata's whistling.
He's over a block away
When I hear him coming
Carrying the melody.

When he sees me
He isn't surprised—or pleased.
And neither am I, yet I say,
"I've found you, Tata!"
A line I've practiced for days.
For months.
Tata's whistle I recognize,
But I don't recognize Tata.

He has a weak beard,
Which stops him from smiling,
And he is thin.

He looks at the woman,
Who says, "I know."
But what does she know?

She takes the child upstairs
And I hear crying—
Coming from the woman,
Not from the child.

Tata leads me to the large kitchen
And makes hot chocolate
Using a clean, steel kettle.
"It is a hard thing to explain—
        to a child," he says,
Without looking at me
To see how much I've grown.

I don't listen much.
His little bee-sting words
Hurt.

Tata peels an orange,
The skin coming away
In one expert movement
Creating a bitter coil
On the counter.
He splits the orange in two,
Rests one half before me,
Eats the other half himself,
Pips and all.
Tata looks at the clock above the sink.

The hot chocolate is untouched
And cold
In the cup.

I am cold too
So I stand to leave.

"Will you come and see Mama?" I ask.
Tata looks at the clock again
And says,
    In English,
        "Eventually."

Blame

My stomach tightens into a rock
Because I am so angry with Tata.

Every time Mama looks at
Her map on the wall—
Every time Mama pulls on
Her coat and walking shoes—
Every time Mama opens up
Her purse and frowns—
Every time Mama comes to
Bed and lies awake weeping.

I am so angry that
My stomach is a stone
I wish I could throw at Tata.

A Letter I Never Send

Tata,

We came to Coventry to find you,
Mama and me.
We looked and looked.

Now you know we are here
I'm not looking,
I'm waiting.
I don't want to wait and wait,
what's the point?

Mama loves you again;
she's sorry.
Can't you be sorry too?
Then we can go back to Babcia,
*   back to Gdańsk,*
*   home.*

Please, Tata.

Kasienka

The Bell Jar

It was in the senior section
     of the library.
I liked the fuchsia cover. I liked her name.
Plath. A name like a heavy breath.

And I read. Slowly I read. In English.
About Plath's desire to die.

And I wonder if I could do that.
I wonder if I could surrender.

And take my last breaths
Instead of living with a rock
In my belly.

Skin Deep

"She isn't even pretty,"
    I tell Kanoro.

We are shelling peas for dinner,
Popping more into our mouths
Than we put in the pan.

"She isn't as pretty as Mama,"
    I tell him.

Kanoro isn't surprised.
He shakes his head.

He sees Mama's grace,
And sometimes he creates it.

"And the child isn't as pretty as you,"
    Kanoro says.

He knows this will make me cry,
Which I do.

I Didn't Mean to Go Back

To see Tata,
      And Melanie,
      And the baby,
      Briony,
Who is my sister,
Although they haven't said so,
And I don't ask.

It just happened,
      Quite naturally,
      And I never
      Mention it

To Mama.

Something draws me.

It isn't the hot chocolate;
I never can finish a cup.
It isn't the monstrous television;
It only ever plays cartoons.

It is, maybe, the calm family feel
Of the kitchen,

Where Melanie
Throws food into the microwave,

Clothes into the washing machine,
Going about her chores with pleasure—ease—
And not complaining, or too tired to play
With the baby
Or talk to me
When Tata's not around.

Melanie

I don't want her to be nice.
It isn't her job.

And it makes me feel wicked
When she offers me a piece of cheesecake,
More than I could possibly eat,
With as much whipped cream as I like.

It would be easier if
She hated me,
Then I wouldn't feel so guilty.

She could turn me away
When I stand at
        The doorstep
Hungry and tired—
The out-of-date daughter.

She doesn't do that.
She wouldn't.
Because she's nice.

She makes milk shakes.
Any flavor I like.

She asks about *me*:
About school,
Swimming,

Poland—
        Never about Mama,
Of course.

I don't always respond.
I sulk a lot.
To show her what she is
And what she's done.
But she doesn't seem to notice.
She doesn't expect me to like her.
No moods when
I ignore the child.

And when Tata's around
She leaves us alone.
She knows she isn't welcome,
Isn't a part of this history
                        Or of us.

I want to hate Melanie,
But I can see why Tata wants her.
And sometimes, when Melanie
Leaves the room
I wish she'd stayed,
Because she's easier to be with
Than Tata;

She looks me straight in the eye
Which is more than he can ever do.

The Gospel According to Tata

Tata didn't teach me to lie,
        Now he's condoning it,
Every time I land at his door
        And he doesn't mention Mama.
Every time he offers me money
        To pay for my silence.
Tata took me to church
        Though I protested some Sundays
Because virtue matters,
        He'd said.
Tata taught me prayers
        That took hours to recite—
The holy rosary and
        How to hold the beads,
To count the prayers,
        Do daily worship.
Tata wrote the rules
        We had to follow—
Rules he never read
        Himself.
Tata's ashamed
        Whenever he has to see me
And be reminded of the sin
        He never planned to commit.

Lady Godiva

The long-haired Lady Godiva rode naked
As a new lamb
Through the Saxon streets of Coventry.

Her husband should have loved her more.
He should have loved her enough to
Concede,
To keep her safe from Peeping Tom.

Now, in Broadgate,
There is a statue, a misplaced tribute
Outside a coffee shop.

And no one stops to look up
At the brave, bronze Lady Godiva,
Who cared more for others
Than for her own modesty,
Apart from the odd teenage boy
Who doesn't really look at Godiva
But at something else,
And misses the point completely.

Ready

Mama listens to *Madame Butterfly* and
Sings along to "Un Bel Di Vedremo."
When she hits a high note,
One only she can reach,
She raises her hands
Like a soprano on stage at
The Grand Theatre.

She is so bold
I imagine she is capable of anything.

So I tell her the truth.

She shuts off the music,
Sits on the bed and twists her
Hands in her lap.

I see she is seething,
But her mouth stays still
While I tell her everything
                Except who found Tata.
And then she says,
"You should have told me sooner.
Do you think Mama is an idiot?
This woman must think Mama is an idiot.
Tata thinks Mama is an idiot too.

It's Tata and Kasienka now,
Isn't it?"

I want to tell her that it will
Never be Tata and Kasienka—
It's true, Tata doesn't want her,
But he doesn't want me either.

Mama is up and out the door
Before I can defend myself,
Before I can beg her to stay,
Before I can say "I love you

The Most."

Guilty

We are playing Scrabble,
Staring at plastic squares and
Pretending to practice our English,
Permitting Polish and Swahili,
When Mama returns.

We know where she's been because
Her face is swollen,
And she cannot speak.

Kanoro stands and moves to the door,
But Mama puts a hand out to stop him.

Stay.

"Stay," I say,
Holding on to Kanoro's shirttail.

He brews Mama a drink
With something in it to help her play
Scrabble without wheezing.

Mama can't look at me,
Even when I set down a long word.

I am glad Kanoro is here.
I wouldn't have known

What to do with Mama
When she came home
All mixed up,
Like the letters in the Scrabble bag,
Carrying with her a terrible sadness
And showing it off so
Unashamedly.

Motherless

Mama is so angry with me.
White,
Light,
Silent anger.

She cooks my meals,
Washes my clothes,
Sleeps next to me at night.

But Mama slams the pots
So I can hear her anger,
And burns the stews
So I can smell it,

And she avoids my eyes;
Not an easy thing to do
When we live together
In one room.

She looks at me sometimes.

Sometimes I catch her looking.

And when I do
She turns away—
Slowly,
Deliberately.
        Enraged.

When I tell her I made
The swim team
She still won't look.

She won't look at me when I sit
Opposite her at dinner
Trying not to spill anything,
Even eating the onions.

She won't look at me
In bed at night,
And if we accidentally touch,
She shakes me off like
She's been bitten,
Like I'm poison.

So now I'm feeling too
Brittle to look at her.

Instead I stare at the
Hem of her dress,

Or a clip in her hair,
Or the rings on her fingers
When we speak.

And it all makes me feel
Like going swimming.

Desperation

It is
Not my fault
Tata doesn't
Love you
Anymore.

Can I say that to her?

Hope

Someone was cruel to Mama at work.
"Sorry," I say.
Mama sniffs.

And now she wants to go home.
"To Gdańsk?" I ask.
She nods.

She hasn't showered in days.
"Really?" I ask.
She nods again.

"When?" I ask.
Mama shrugs.

Then puts her head into her hands and weeps.

Split

There are many Kasienkas now.

She has split into pieces and
Scattered herself about like fallen fruit
Beneath a leafless tree.

One Kasienka is Mama's girl—
The Kasienka who chews quietly
And sleeps with a teddy bear in her arms.
She is muted and hidden and
Wants nothing more than to run to Tata—
To form a real family again.

Another Kasienka is Tata's pilgrim,
The tight-lipped teenage Kasienka.
She is frightening and moody.

She is also William's Cassie,
Shy eyed and broad backed—
A swimmer, but a girl before anything else:
A girlfriend with a mouth and breasts.

Cassie belongs to Clair too,
She smells of cabbage and fear.

She is a dumb, defiant victim.
But she is easily demolished.

If only I knew Kasienka's Kasienka:

When I search for myself in the bathroom mirror
I cannot find her at all.

When I am alone
I do not know who I am.

When I am alone
I am nothing.

PART 3

Dalilah

You are the new girl in the class
And maybe they will hate you
    Instead of me.

They do it like this:
They look,
    They whisper,
        They laugh.
And it doesn't sound like much,
But when it happens
    Every day
It feels like you're walking uphill
Carrying a giant boulder on your shoulders.

You are the new girl in the class
And maybe they will hate you
    Instead of me.

Maybe they will notice your shoes.
I do.
    They are not like everyone else's:
They are thick and buckled
    And you're wearing knee-high socks
Which no one does.

But I only half want that—
I only half want you hunted.

Mostly I want a friend.

So when the teacher says,
"Lily will need a partner,"
I throw up my hand,
Offer up myself to you,

And you look at me and smile
And that
      Makes
      My
      Day.

The Veil

Dalilah wears a purple veil and she is so pretty in it.
She is
      All eyes.

I make myself jealous looking at her,
Imagining my face framed,
My hair hidden beneath folds of fabric.

When I see women in the street
With veils down to their feet,
Chadors,
I am jealous too.
Jealous of their concealment,
Of a robe that would cover me
                    from head to toe
And hide me from the world.

It would be like a kind of armor,
A veil like that,
A veil that covered me
                    from head to toe
So no one could get in.

July 7

At 8:50 a.m. the Bell rings and we stand
To remember
What happened
In London.

But Clair is looking at Dalilah
Forgetting,
Not remembering at all.

And at break we are surrounded
And Marie says,
"Why did you say they deserved it?
I heard you. I heard you whisper to Cassie.
I heard you say that."

And Dalilah looks at me because she was
Standing to remember
What we were all too young to remember
While Clair was standing looking at her.

In Mama's Absence

There are balloons all over the place.
There are red balloons in the house
And more in the garden.
Helium balloons on strings
To keep them from being
Captured by the sky.

William's grandmother
Is having her birthday party
And she wanted balloons
Instead of waxy candles that would
Ruin the cake.

There is a barbecue in the garden
And William's father
Is wearing a striped apron and
Cooking everything outside.
Meats mainly.

There is music
Coming from two heavy black
Speakers
Connected to an iPod
And a bouncy castle for the kids.

We both want to bounce
But his cousins are on it and they're

Young—
And we don't want to
Be like them.

Then William's grandmother
Crawls into the castle and starts to jump
                                    And jump

And I laugh
Out loud
With William.
I do not think she is like
Any grandmother
I have ever seen before.
I could not imagine Babcia
Bouncing.

So it's okay for us to jump
Too.
And we do.
We hold hands and jump and jump
And I squeal a little
When I fall over,
When I fall on top of William,
Which I do
Again
And again.

William's father doesn't scowl

When we close
The bedroom door,
Just says, "Be good, kids."

William turns on his computer
And asks me to choose a song.
I point to a track I don't recognize
And he says, "Cool,"
And I feel good.

Music fills the small room as
A firework explodes inside my belly and
Color spins and sparkles in my gut.

When he smiles it is like having a torch
Shine right at me
        Lighting up all the dark corners,
And I cannot imagine why everyone
Is not in love with him.

William leans in,
Opens his mouth
And I do too.
But not too wide.
Just enough
To give him room to breathe into me.

I close my eyes,
Let William lead,

And try not to pant too loudly
As we do things
      Mama would hate.

When we have kissed enough
I ask him where his mother is—
Why his mother is missing—
And he shows me a photograph
Of a woman with no hair and says
"Mom died."

And then we hug
Until it is very dark outside.

And I tell him how sorry I am.
And I tell him about Mama
And Tata,

And revealing our feelings
Means more than the kisses ever could.

And inside I am bursting to tell Tata how grateful
I am that he was missing and
Not dead.

Maybe I Should Not

Be thinking of William
And aching
    In this way.

But when Mama sees me and
Doesn't look closely enough to notice the scandal
Printed all over my skin,

    I do not feel guilty at all.

Confidence

When I tell William
      All about Clair
He says, "Stand up for yourself."

William is in eighth grade.
He could save me from the pack
But he does not want to:
      He knows
      I can save
      Myself.

And this makes me glow
And love him even more.

Practice

Girls shouldn't want to
Beat each other—
But I want to beat everyone,

To know I'm faster,
And stronger
Than the girls in the other lanes,
Than Clair in lane four.

It isn't meant to be a competition.
We're just training.

No prizes or trophies for coming in first
Today.

And yet.

When I hear the whistle,
I dive with a fierceness
I don't expect,
And a passion for first place
Propels me
Through the water
To the other end and back again.

I take breaths
Only every four strokes,

Preferring to see the
Blinking tiled bottom of the pool
Than the clumsy splashes
Of my teammates,
Than Clair out ahead of me.

When I pull myself from the pool
Ms. Morrow approaches and says,
                              "Nice one."

Then, one after another,
The other girls emerge too.
Some shake their heads,
Others prefer to cut their eyes.
Clair won't look,
She turns in the water
And backstrokes
To the other end.

"She wants to be team captain,"
Marie tells me later.
"So be careful;
There'll be trouble if the coach
Chooses you."

Ms. Morrow

Ms. Morrow does not know.
She does not know but she suspects.

After practice she keeps me back
To check.

And this is what I have been waiting for.

But I do not know what to say.
Or how to tell what's happened.

When Ms. Morrow says, "What's going on?"
I cannot tell her everything.

So I tell her nothing.

Family

When Mama and Tata stand together
They do not look right:
Tata is too shiny for the room
      And for Mama
Now.

Together they are tuneless;
The sounds they make are ugly,
Like knives being sharpened
Against stone.

Together they are waxwork statues;
Recognizable
      But lifeless.

Tata will not look around the room
Even when Mama says,
"Look!
      Look where we have been living!"
He is staring at his smart, shiny
Shoes and will not notice
There is only one bed in the room
And the kitchen is in here too.

"Look!
      Look how we have been living!"
Mama shouts.

But Tata is staring at his tight, shiny
Shoes and will not notice
That Mama's clothes are frayed and frumpy
And mine are too.

Tata merely mumbles and goes on
Looking at the floor
While Mama keeps condemning him.

Tata is as silent in the room
As he was before we found him.

When Tata has gone Mama whispers,
"Look . . .
    Look at what your father has become.
    And Kasienka
    loves Tata
    more than
    she loves
    Mama."

A Solution

Melanie is standing at the school gates
    holding Briony
    by the hand.
Briony is wearing a green dress
    and licking a melting ice cream cone.

Melanie waves and I wave back
    and then we walk
    together to her car
Where she buckles Briony in
    and Briony rubs ice cream
    all over the seats.

Melanie is taking Briony to the pool
    And thinks I might like to come too,
    Which I do.

I do not do laps up
              And down
The pool because
The wave machine is on so I splash
    And play with Briony
    And we pretend we are at the beach,
    The wild ocean lapping us,
    Launching us onto the shore.

Melanie does not change into her swimsuit;

She sits by the side of the pool
Chat, chat, chatting on her phone
And not watching us at all.

So when a wave takes Briony away from the edge
        Into the gyre of water
                And spins
                Her
                About
                And around
                Up and down,
Melanie will not save her because she is
        Chat, chat, chatting on the phone.
        And for a moment I pause
        And wonder what life could be without
        Briony.

Allegiance

When Tata gets home from work we sit
Around the dining table
      Like a real family
Eating spaghetti bolognese,
Wearing bibs like babies, and
Trying not to flick sauce on our faces.

Melanie says, "She was amazing.
               She saved her life."

Then Melanie says,
      "We would like you to come and live with us,
      Kasienka. Here."

I stop eating my pasta to look at Tata,
      To see if this means he has left Mama
      Forever.

And Melanie says,
      "You would have your own bed.
      You would have a room to yourself
      And a computer, if you like."

Tata has been telling tales,
Stories that make Mama
      seem bad.

When he looks up he is frowning
>And then he looks at Briony
>And I know this means that he will not be back
>To live with us;
That it is Melanie and Briony
Forever.

She serves éclairs for dessert,
>Expensive chocolate-dribbled pastries
That Mama could never afford,
And I wish I could take mine home.
To give to Mama.
As a treat.
Instead of eating it
Myself.

When I am helping to load the dishes
>Melanie takes my arm and says,
>"Will you come and live with us?"

But Melanie does not know
How Mama would feel.

"No," I say. "I can't live here."

I won't leave Mama.

Cracked

I cannot make Mama whole again.
Tata stole
 pieces
 of
 her
And now she is
 Jagged at the edges—
 Cracked.

When I get home I take off my shoes
To keep the carpet clean
And do my homework
Without asking questions.

I tiptoe.
I am silent.

She does not look at me
Anymore.

She lies in bed
With a book and a
Glass of wine
Held to her heart.

Sometimes she drinks
     Half a bottle,

And maybe she drinks
    Even more.

And then she goes to sleep
Without saying
    good night,
Without turning off the light,
Without checking I'm all right.

Sleepover

We devour too many licorice laces,
Too many cans of Coke
And buckets of popcorn,
So when we try to sleep
It's impossible;
We keep thinking of funny things
To tell each other
And secrets to share,
Stories we forgot were important
Until we turned out the lights.

When I admit the reason Dalilah cannot
Sleep over at my house,
When I tell her there would be
      Three people
      In one bed
      If she stayed,
She says, "I used to sleep with Grandma
When I was little. It wasn't so bad."

She does not feel sorry
Or come closer to comfort me:
Instead
She tells her own secrets
And they are just as strange
As mine.

And I do not feel sorry either.

When the birds start fidgeting,
When the darkness has lifted,
We are still awake
And cannot imagine sleeping
With so much on our minds.

So we go downstairs for breakfast.

Cooking Stones

Ms. Morrow says I'm the
Best swimmer in seventh grade,
Maybe in Coventry.
She wants me to come with
The team to a swim meet
In London
In two weeks,
     To race
Against girls who
Could beat me.

Schools from across the country
Are competing.
Ms. Morrow gives me a blank permission slip
To take home.

Mama shakes her head:
No. Absolutely. No.

She doesn't give a reason.
She doesn't have to.
The reason is clear:
I don't deserve it.

    Kanoro says:
"Patience can cook a stone."

I know he means I need to give Mama time.
I know he means she'll stop blaming me
When she's feeling well again.
I know he means other things too.

But I am thirteen and
Mama's forty-two,
So she should know better.

Isn't that what they say?
She should know better.

Good News

Kanoro received special papers,
So he's going to work in London
At a place called St. Bart's,
As an actual doctor
        For children.

When he tells Mama and me
He is so excited
He knocks over a lamp and
Rubs out the light.

Mama doesn't care about the lamp:
For the first time in a month
She laughs
        and runs to hug Kanoro.

My feelings are untidy:
I am happy
        to see Mama this way,
I am sad
        Kanoro must leave,

And I am confused:
I don't know why they are both
So thrilled
When Kanoro's news
Means he will leave us.

Vacant

I tell him
     not to warn me.

I do not want
     to say good-bye.

I am used to lost
     Good-byes.

And so,
     One day,
          When I get home,

His door is open,
His bed is stripped,
His books are gone,
His room is empty.

And I change my mind:
I want to say good-bye
After all.

Rebellion

William says I should go to London
Anyway.

He doesn't always do what
He's told.
"No one does," he tells me,
Kissing me,
Showing me.

We walk past my bus stop
And I don't go straight home
To Mama.

"I've lied too much already,"
I say.
And he says,

"Then what's one more?"

And this is true.
What harm can it do,
To lie
Just once more?

Betrayal

When I go to Tata's house,
To ask him to sign the slip—
He's my parent too
After all—
He isn't there;
It's just Melanie and the child.

So I plead with her to sign.
And she does,
With a blunt pencil
From Briony's toy box.

Then she takes a
Coloring book,
And on the back
Copies down the date.
"I'll tell your father,"
She says.

Every day after school
I train for the competition;
Every day I am cleansed
By this daily baptism.
Every day I am swallowed and saved.

Mama doesn't care
Where I am anymore.

She's happy to have lost me
To the water.

Lies in the Dark

Mama is asleep when I
                Tiptoe out
                Of our room
With my bag in one hand
My permission slip in the other.
I packed my bag last night,
And hid it under the kitchen sink.

I leave a note, so she won't worry,
A lie scratched out in the dark
About an open house at the school.

From the bus stop
I can see our window,
And I wish Mama would appear
And wave good-bye.
Good-bye and good luck.

She doesn't, of course.
Mama's groaning in her sleep,
Groaning and dreaming of
Tata and Kasienka
Plotting against her.

To London

Some rules are universal:
The back of the bus is reserved for the popular.

So I'm at the front behind Ms. Morrow.
And William is somewhere in the middle
With the other older boys,
Huddled around a phone watching YouTube.

The back is where Clair sits,
Surrounded by a horde of wild approval.
They actually applaud when she boards the bus,
A smattering of claps and hoots
Like echoes in a jungle.
She smiles shyly, fakes embarrassment,
And looks past me for once.

Ms. Morrow turns around and says, "Excited?"
I pretend not to have heard
And take a book from my bag
Because I have already told
My last lie.

Fear

The echoes—the shouts and splashes,
Carry through to the changing room
Where I am pulling on my
Nearly-not-there swimsuit.

The girls in my race are taller
And leaner, with polished toenails and shaved legs
And I am not sure I will be able to get myself
        out of the changing room
And into the pool at all
If everyone's looking.

Clair appears from a cubicle
        in her own swimsuit,
More womanly
Than all the rest—
Her breasts round,
Her nipples quiet—
And she wishes me luck
By tousling my short hair.

Now I know there's only one way
To get Revenge.

Starting Blocks

The cheering and chants
From the throbbing crowd
Fade to nothing
When I'm on the
Block.
I only hear an underwater din,
A ringing, babbling vacuum,
And a kind of coaxing
Coming from the water.

In the bright light the people look
Like ghosts, and then I see one—Tata—
Standing up in the crowd,
Quiet and stern, as focused as I am.

And then I spot William too,
Holding up a sign with my name on it.

There isn't time to check whether they're real
Or phantoms in my mind.

There isn't time to check for Mama.

We're on our marks.

Ready.
Set.
Go.

Home

Water is another world:
A land with its own language

Which I speak fluently.

It's alien and dangerous.
I can't even breathe down here.

Treading water
Works only if I relax;
If I fight,
          I sink.
I have to trust myself,
Trust the territory and
My own body,
The power of each limb.

It's the silence I want.

And the weight of the water
Over me—
          Around me—
The safe silence of submergence.

At the pool's edge I might be ugly,
But when I speak strokes

I am beautiful.

Gold

Tata hugs me when I finish
Even though I am wet
And he's wearing a suit.

"My Olympian," he says,
And looks so proud
I couldn't care less

Who sees me crying.

Metamorphosis

Clair tears open my cubicle door
Without knocking,
But I am already fully dressed.

"You think you're something,"
She barks.
There are two girls behind her
But they are far enough away
For me to know they won't interfere.
I step close to Clair and whisper,
In a language I think she'll understand,
"Why don't you just piss off."
The girls behind her giggle and
Clair gapes, about to retaliate,
When suddenly she sees my joy,
My win,
And her power dissolves.

The two girls cough and step away
And Clair is left
To face me unsupported,
Which she cannot do.

"Whatever," she says and
Turns, runs, shouts—
"Wait for me!"

Forgiveness

Mama does not know how to say sorry,
But now that Kanoro has gone
She is lonelier than me,
And much quieter,
So quiet I sometimes check that she
Hasn't died of heartache.

With Kanoro gone
And Tata gone
Maybe Mama is unhappier
Than I can understand.

When she sees the trophy,
A golden swimmer
Diving from a marble platform
Into space, she says,
"It wasn't your fault, Kasienka,"
And that's as much as she can admit,
Or as happy as she can be for me.

And for now, that's okay.

Reunion

I am sitting on the
Front steps of our
Building, chewing gum
Waiting for William,
When Kanoro arrives
Without warning.

I jump up to greet him
And he takes me
Into his arms without embarrassment.

"Where's the birthday girl?" he asks.

Mama was standing at our window
Watching me and is down the stairs
Before I have a chance to answer.

Mama runs to Kanoro.

They look stupid together:
Mama is bright white.
Kanoro is too black against her.
And yet, the picture is pretty good.

Treat

Kanoro takes Mama to dinner.
She wears a yellow dress
And shoes so high
She wobbles when she walks.

Mama wore that dress once before,
In Gdańsk,
When Tata took her to the theater
And they came home
Holding hands.

But Mama and Kanoro
Are not hand holding
When they get back from dinner
At all.

They are holding their tummies
Because they ate too many
Tacos.

And then they are holding their sides
Laughing.

Kanoro sleeps on the couch
And in the morning,
After tea and toast,
He honks his horn,

Waves from the window of his
New car, and disappears
Onto the ring road.

I watch Mama closely,
Afraid she will rearrange herself
Into grief.

"People usually come back, Mama,"
I say, and she nods

As she folds the sheer yellow dress and
Lays it neatly in a drawer.

"I think I need a haircut," she says.

Resurrection

Mama is alive again,
A little bit alive.

She isn't singing.
But now and then she
Hums
Without meaning to.

Side by Side

Clair still stands in the center
Surrounded by a thick circle of girls.

I can feel their desperation,
The thirst for admission.

It is a dance for popularity,
Swapping places every day,
Knowing that tomorrow
Any one of them could be

                             out.

Maybe it's lonely for Clair
                   There
          In the center
Directing the dance.

She ignores me again,
Which is better than being bullied.

Dalilah and I stand together
                         Side by side.
There is no one in the center,
We're just looking out
In the same direction
Not desperately at each other
Fearing betrayal.

EPILOGUE

Butterfly

Now that I can front crawl,
Back crawl,
Breaststroke,

I am breaking out.
Ms. Morrow is teaching me
        The butterfly.

When I am in the water
My body moves like a wave:
There is a violence to it
And a beauty.

I lie on my chest,
My arms outstretched
My legs extended back—
Waiting to kick.

And I pull,
            Push,
                    Recover.
This is how the Butterfly works.

I have to hollow out spaces
For breathing,
And if I miss them
I can't swim.

But I do.
I know when to come up for air,
When to keep my head down.

At practice,
On the starting block
I am not frightened at all:

I am standing on my own,
And it
Never felt so good.

Glossary

mama—mom
tata—dad
babcia—grandma
Gdańsk—a seaport city in Poland
Gdańsk Główny—a train station in Gdańsk
pierogi—boiled dumplings of unleavened dough,
    often stuffed with potato
bigos—traditional Polish stew
golabki—stuffed cabbage rolls

Acknowledgments

This book might never have found the light were it not for several special people: my agent, the wonderful Julia Churchill, who worked tirelessly to read, edit, and champion the project; everyone at Bloomsbury, especially my editor, Ele Fountain, for her hard work, insight, and sensitivity; the Edward Albee Foundation (its founder and fellows), which gave me the space and time to complete this novel; my friends and early readers, Erin Whitcraft and Jill Wehler; the Hudson School, notably its principal and founder, Suellen Newman, who has always been a remarkable source of support and inspiration; and Marta Gut for her invaluable cultural advice on Poland.

Many books influenced my writing, and it would be impractical to mention them all, but I would like to highlight *Odd Girl Out* by Rachel Simmons, which informed so much of my understanding about girls and bullying.

I am especially grateful to Mum, Dad, Jimmy, and Andreas for their love and support.

WHAT CAN'T BE FORGIVEN?

MOONRISE

SARAH CROSSAN

BLOOMSBURY

THE FIRST CALL

The green phone
on the wall in the hall
hardly ever rang.
Anyone who wanted to speak to Mom called her cell.
Same with Angela.

I listened to the jangle for a few seconds
before picking it up.
"Hello?"

"Joe?" It was Ed.
He hadn't been in touch for weeks.
I'd started to worry,
wondered if he was ever coming home.
"Is Angela there?" he asked.
He was breathing fast
as though someone were chasing him.
In the background
  hard voices,
   a door slamming.

"Angela's at soccer practice," I said.

"And Mom?"

"No idea.
Hey, Ed,
I found a baseball glove at the park.
Will you be back soon to play?"

Ed sighed heavily. "I dunno, Joe."

"Oh." I picked at some peeling paint on the wall.

Another sigh from my big brother.
"I got arrested, Joe.
They think I done something real bad."

I pressed the receiver tight
            against my ear.
"What do they think you done?"

"They think I hurt someone.
But I didn't. You hear?"

"Yeah."

"I mean it. You hear me?
'Cause people are gonna be telling you
all kinds of lies.
I need you to know the truth."

The front door opened and Mom stormed in
carrying a bag of groceries
for my sister to conjure into dinner.

"The police got Ed!" I shouted.

 I held out the phone.
  She snatched it from me,
  dropping the bag.

A tangerine rolled across the rug.
I picked it up,
the skin cold and rough.

"Ed? What's going on? . . .
But how can they make that sort of mistake? . . .
Don't shout at me, I'm just . . .
No, I know, but . . .
I don't have the money for . . .
Ed, stay calm . . .
I'll call Karen. I said I'll call Karen . . .
Stop shouting at me . . .
Ed, for Christ's sake . . .
I'm just not able to . . . Ed? Ed?"

She held the phone away
              from her ear and scowled
              like it had bitten her.
"The cops are charging him with murder," she said.

I was seven.
I didn't know what that meant.
Did he owe someone money?
We didn't have any cash to pay the electricity bill.
My sneakers were so small
they made the tips of my toes white.
"Can I call him back?" I asked.
The tangerine was still in my hand.
I wanted to throw it in Mom's face and hurt her.

"No," she said.
"And don't expect to speak to him for a long time."

I didn't believe her.
I thought Ed would call.
I thought he'd come home.

But he never did.

SLUM LANDLORD

Aunt Karen told me not to come here.
She said Ed didn't deserve an entourage
after the pain he'd caused our family.

Even after ten long years
she blames him for everything.
       She points to Ed and says,
        "See what he did to us."

And maybe she's right.
Everything turned to shit
when Ed got put away;
nothing worked anymore.

So maybe this *is* a stupid idea.

I'm already pining for home, Staten Island,
anything that isn't Wakeling, Texas,
in the broiling heat.

It's not as if I *want* to be here,
checking out some slummy apartment.
But I can't afford to keep staying at
the Wakeling Motorstop Motel,
not for the whole time I'm in Texas, anyway.

"Six hundred for the month," the landlord croaks,
coughing up something wet and
spitting it into a Kleenex.

Judging by the dishes in the sink,
the apartment hasn't been lived in for months, and
he'd be lucky to get a dime for this hole—
roaches in the closets,
rodents in the kitchen.

"I need it until mid-August.
I'll give you four hundred," I say.

He snorts. "Five hundred. Cash."
And I can tell by the way he's
        backing out of the apartment
            that it's as low as he'll go.
Well, I guess he's the one with the keys;
he can afford to play hardball.
"If I find out you been selling weed,
I'll send my men around.
You don't wanna meet my men."

But his men don't bother me.
I got bigger worries
        than getting bashed in with a baseball bat
by his hired goons.

I got Ed to worry about.
        Ed.

So here I am.
        Stuck.

And it's going to be the worst time of my life.
The worst time of everyone's lives.

        For those who get to live.

TEXTS

In the parking lot of my motel
a gang of bikers is slugging booze from paper bags,
hellfire rock music filling up the lot.

As I pass them, my cell phone pings in my
back pocket.
I don't bother checking the message.
I know it's Angela pestering me:

> Where r u?
> Did u go 2 the prison?
> U seen Ed??
> Hows Ed???
> Karens still srsly pissed off.
> Eds new lawyer emailed. He seems smart.
> Where R U???

I have to call my sister.
And I will.
> Later.
Right now, I'm starving.

And I have to get away from this music.

BOB'S DINER

The diner is all beat up outside,
paint crumbling, half the neon sign unlit,
and inside it's the same:
broken floor tiles,
posters pale and torn.
A middle-aged waitress in a
pink bowling shirt smiles.
Her name—"Sue"—is embroidered into
her front pocket,
the black thread unraveling itself,
        snaking down the shirt like a
        little vine.

"You okay, hon?" she asks,
raising her hand to her mouth,
dragging on a cigarette right there
behind the counter
like it's totally normal—
        a waitress smoking in a restaurant.
And it might be.   Around here.

I pull out my remaining cash and wave it at her.
"What would four bucks buy me?" I say.

"I guess you could get a BLT
and a coffee.
Would that work, hon?"

"Great," I say, inhaling the
        tail of her cigarette smoke.

She shouts my order through a swinging door,
turns back to slosh coffee into a stained mug,
        and pushes it across the counter.

It's thick and bitter, nothing like you get in
New York,
but I don't complain.
        I tear open a Splenda
                tip it in to disguise the taste.
"Any jobs available?" I ask.

        "Wait there, hon."
Sue vanishes
        through the
swinging doors.

I grab a muffin in plastic wrap from a basket
on the counter, stuff it into my bag before
        a man appears,

a thick mustache hiding his mouth,
a belly that bulges over his waistband.

He reaches across the counter, shakes my hand.
"I'm Bob. I believe you're lookin' for work."
His accent is drawn out and totally Texan.

"Joe Moon," I say.

He nods.
"I need a delivery guy.
Someone with a car, 'cause the junker
out back won't run.
Or someone real fast on a bike.
The fast person would also need a bike."

"I fix cars," I say quickly.
"If I get it to run, could I have the job?"

Sue has reappeared, a fresh cigarette limp
        between her twiggy fingers.
She spits bits of tobacco onto the floor.
"Just so's you know, hon, my boyfriend Lenny's
good with motors. Even he couldn't get that
crap heap to turn over."

She uses a sour rag
to wipe coffee stains from the countertop.

"I could try," I say,
not wanting to sound too desperate.

"Okay. You can *try*," Bob says.
He reaches into the basket and
hands me a blueberry muffin.
"Dessert's on me, son," he says.

NO SHORE

All last week
Reed tried to cheer me up.
Sitting in his car drinking warm beer,
he tried to make me believe Ed would get off,
that I'd be back in Arlington before
the summer track meet
began.
"I'll win bronze for the four-hundred-meter hurdles,
you'll get a gold for the five thousand meters.
Then we'll go to the shore
and show off our medals.
We can stay at my cousin's beach house
as long as we want.
We'll get tans,
        smoke dope,
              hit on hot girls.
So many hot girls at the shore."

"Sounds good," I said,
knowing it was never gonna happen,
knowing I'd miss out on my entire
summer,
including the New York City
track meet.

It was the one thing that had kept me going
in school—
        knowing that at the end of the year,
        no matter how low my grades were,
        I'd have the meet to prove
        I wasn't some layabout loser.

But instead of running,
I was coming to Texas
to count down the days until
my brother's execution;
trying to make me feel better about that
was pointless.